For Jenny, Kate and Hannah Whiteway –
may all your Christmas wishes come true!

Special thanks to
Narinder Dhami

ORCHARD BOOKS
338 Euston Road, London NW1 3BH
Orchard Books Australia
Hachette Children's Books
Level 17/207 Kent Street, Sydney, NSW 2000
A Paperback Original

First published in 2007 by Orchard Books

HiT entertainment

A CIP catalogue record for this book is
available from the British Library.

ISBN 978 1 84616 506 1
5 7 9 10 8 6
Printed in Great Britain

Orchard Books is a division of Hachette Children's Books,
an Hachette Livre UK company.
www.hachettelivre.co.uk

Chrissie
the Wish Fairy

by Daisy Meadows

ORCHARD BOOKS

www.rainbowmagic.co.uk

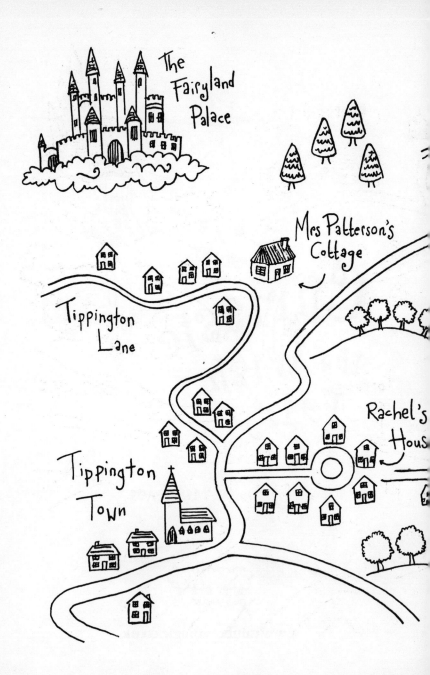

The Fairyland Palace

Mrs Patterson's Cottage

Tippington Lane

Rachel's House

Tippington Town

Christmas
Card Crisis

Goblins, do as I command,
And go right now to the human land.
Search high, search low, search everywhere
For fairy items hidden there.

Christmas wishes won't come true,
If you do as I ask of you.
Find Chrissie's magic items soon –
Magic Card, Carol Sheet and Spoon.

Contents

Postbox Surprise

"Kirsty, it's snowing!" Rachel Walker exclaimed with delight as she opened the front door.

Kirsty Tate, Rachel's best friend, peered outside to see large snowflakes falling steadily.

"Brilliant!" Kirsty beamed, picking up her gloves. "I hope it's snowing back home, too."

Kirsty was staying with Rachel in Tippington for a few days before returning home on Christmas Eve.

"Maybe we're going to have a white Christmas!" Rachel sighed happily, wrapping her scarf snugly round her neck and picking up the bundle of Christmas cards her mum had asked her to post. "Come on, Kirsty. The postbox isn't far."

The two girls went outside. The air was crisp and clear, although it was freezing cold.

"Doesn't everything look different when it's covered with snow?" Kirsty remarked, as they walked down the street.

"Yes, it looks so beautiful and sparkly," Rachel agreed, glancing at the leafless trees. The branches were now layered with snow.

"Almost as beautiful as Fairyland!" Kirsty added happily. The two girls knew all about Fairyland because they

had visited it many times! Rachel and Kirsty were friends with the fairies, and they often helped out their tiny, magical friends when they were in trouble.

"Let's hope Jack Frost and his goblins don't cause any trouble this Christmas," Rachel said as they reached the postbox at the end of the street. Kirsty nodded. "Maybe Jack Frost's decided to enjoy Christmas this year," she said hopefully, as Rachel stepped forward to post the cards through the slot.

Suddenly Rachel gave a little scream. "Kirsty, look!"

Kirsty could hardly believe her eyes. Five knobbly green fingers had emerged from the postbox slot. In an instant the cards were snatched from Rachel's hand and the green fingers had disappeared inside the box again, taking the cards with them.

"There's a goblin inside this postbox!" Rachel declared in horror. "And he's just stolen my Christmas cards!"

Kirsty peered through the slot. It was too dark to see anything, but she could hear rustling noises and the sound of envelopes being torn open.

"No, this isn't it!" the goblin was muttering. "And it's not this one either!" He heaved a loud sigh.

"I think the goblin's looking for something in the envelopes," Kirsty whispered to Rachel.

"Yes, but what?" Rachel wondered.

Before Kirsty could reply, Rachel's Christmas cards suddenly flew out of the slot and landed in the snow around them. Kirsty and Rachel stared at each other in shock.

"What is he doing?" Rachel cried.

"I don't know, but look, there are other envelopes on the ground too," Kirsty pointed out. "It looks like the goblin's been throwing other people's letters out!" She knocked sharply on the postbox. "Hello!" she called through the slot. "What are you doing in there?"

"And why are you throwing people's cards out of the postbox?" Rachel added.

"GO AWAY!" a muffled voice yelled crossly. "I'm hiding! No one's supposed to know I'm here!"

Rachel folded her arms. "We're not moving *one centimetre* until you tell us what you're up to!" she said firmly.

The goblin sighed loudly. "Isn't it obvious?" he snapped. "I'm looking for Chrissie the Wish Fairy's Magic Card!"

Kirsty and Rachel glanced at each other, bewildered. They didn't know anything about a Magic Card.

"We have to get the goblin out of the postbox somehow," Rachel whispered to Kirsty. "We can't have everyone in Tippington finding out about the goblins."

Kirsty nodded solemnly. Anything to do with Fairyland had to be kept completely secret.

"I've got an idea!" Rachel exclaimed suddenly. "We could go to the bakery round the corner and buy some mince pies. Goblins love food. I'm sure he'd come out for a mince pie."

"Great idea!" Kirsty agreed.

The two girls immediately set off. But they'd only gone a few steps when Kirsty noticed a very unusual snowflake drifting down from the sky towards them. It seemed slightly larger than the others and it was twinkling brightly. As Kirsty stared at it more closely, she gave a gasp of wonder.

"Rachel! There's a *fairy* floating down on that snowflake!" she cried, pointing.

Rachel glanced up in amazement and saw a tiny fairy, wearing a white dress trimmed with red, floating gently down towards them.

"Hello, girls!" the fairy called with a little wave. "I'm Chrissie the Wish Fairy!"

Snowflake Special Delivery

As the snowflake drifted past the girls, Chrissie leapt off and hovered in the air in front of them.

"I'm so glad I've found you, girls," Chrissie declared with a beaming smile. "I think I might need your help!"

Rachel and Kirsty glanced excitedly at each other, thinking of the goblin in the postbox.

"I've come to the human world to check that my three magic objects, the Magic Card, the Magic Spoon and the Magic Carol Sheet, are still safely hidden," Chrissie explained. "They are the things that make Christmas wishes come true!"

"Oh!" Rachel gasped. "Chrissie, there's a goblin in that postbox, and he's looking for your Magic Card!"

Chrissie turned pale. "I was afraid of that," she said. "This year, like every Christmas-time, I came to the human world to hide

24

my magic objects. But I've had to
come back again because I know that
Jack Frost has sent his goblins to steal
my magic things!" Chrissie bit her lip,
looking anxious. "I just hope I'm not
too late!"

"How did you find
out that the goblins
were looking for
them?" asked Kirsty.

"You remember my
friend, Holly the Christmas Fairy?" said
Chrissie, and Rachel and Kirsty
nodded. They'd had their very first
Christmas adventure with Holly.

"Well, Holly overheard two goblins
in Santa's workshop saying that Jack
Frost was determined to steal my
magic objects," Chrissie explained.

"They said Jack Frost had already sent a band of goblins to the human world to look for them!"

"What were the goblins doing in Santa's workshop?" Rachel asked curiously.

"Trying to steal the presents," Chrissie replied with a grin. "But Holly soon put a stop to that! Now *I* have to stop the goblins finding my card, my spoon and my carol sheet before Christmas is ruined!"

"How do they work?" Rachel wanted
to know.

"My Magic Card makes sure that
Christmas cards spread Christmas wishes
of joy all around the world," Chrissie
explained. "The magic of my wooden
spoon makes Christmas food taste
lovely, and means that wishes made by
people stirring their Christmas puddings
will be granted."

"And what about the Magic Carol
Sheet?" asked Kirsty.

"That makes sure that carol singers
sing beautifully and can spread
happiness and Christmas wishes without
getting their words mixed up!" Chrissie
replied. "Girls, will you help me keep
my three magic objects safe from Jack
Frost and his goblins?"

27

"Of course we will!" Rachel and Kirsty chorused.

"Thank you so much," Chrissie said, "because we have a bit of a problem." She glanced at the postbox. "You see,

I hid my Magic Card inside that very postbox!" Rachel and Kirsty gasped, but before either of them could say anything, they heard the goblin inside the pillar box shout, "Yippee!"

"Oh, no!" Chrissie groaned, "I think he's found the Magic Card!"

"Maybe he's made a mistake," Kirsty suggested. "There must be lots of Christmas cards in there."

But Chrissie shook her head. "My card is in an envelope that shimmers and glimmers with fairy magic," she explained. "It's impossible to mistake it for an ordinary card."

"We'd better get the goblin out of the postbox then," Rachel pointed out. "Before you arrived, Chrissie, we were thinking of tempting him out with a mince pie."

"That's a good idea," Chrissie agreed. "But we must hurry. You see, anyone holding one of my magic objects can make a wish!"

Kirsty looked dismayed. "You mean the goblin could make a wish while he's got the card?" she asked.

29

Chrissie nodded. "And as long as he makes a *Christmas* wish, then it will come true!" she whispered.

"So the goblin could wish his way back to Jack Frost's ice castle, and take the card with him!" Rachel pointed out anxiously. "We have to get the Magic Card away from the goblin before he figures that out!"

Whoosh!

A shower of glittering golden sparks suddenly shot out of the slot in the postbox, whirled up into the air and then showered down over the pillar box.

Kirsty, Rachel and Chrissie watched in amazement as the postbox began to shake.

"Look!" Rachel cried. "It's *changing*!"

Jingle Bells

The postbox was becoming lower and longer, and its red colour had changed to a glittering gold. Rachel and Kirsty blinked in disbelief as the last few sparks swirled down onto the snow.

A magnificent golden sleigh now stood exactly where the postbox had been.

33

"We're too late!" Chrissie exclaimed, looking upset. "The goblin has already wished for a sleigh to take my Magic Card back to Jack Frost!"

The beautiful sleigh was piled high with silk cushions, and the goblin was lying comfortably on them, looking enormously pleased with himself. The envelopes that had been inside the postbox were now lying on the snowy ground, heaped up around the sleigh.

"There's my Magic Card!" Chrissie whispered. "On that violet cushion next to the goblin!" Rachel and Kirsty looked more closely and spotted a golden envelope shimmering with fairy magic. The envelope had been torn right open and the girls could see a beautiful Christmas card inside. It had a picture of a delicate silver snowflake on the front which glowed and glittered in the frosty air.

Just then the goblin caught sight
of them.

"Ha, a pesky fairy!" he sneered.
"Well, you and your silly human
friends can't catch me. I'm off to Jack
Frost's ice castle, just as soon as I can
work out how to move this stupid
sleigh!" He smirked gleefully at them.
"Take me to Jack Frost's ice castle,
magic sleigh!" he yelled.

The sleigh did
not move.

Chrissie put
a hand over her
mouth to hide
a smile. "The
goblin hasn't realised
yet that he needs something
to *pull* the sleigh!" she whispered.

Grumbling, the goblin jumped to his feet.

"How do I start this thing?" he mumbled, throwing the cushions aside. "Where's the switch?"

"This could be our chance," Chrissie said softly. "Let's try and get the card away from him while he's distracted."

Rachel and Kirsty nodded. They tiptoed over to the sleigh with Chrissie fluttering overhead, their eyes fixed on the shimmering envelope that lay on the violet cushion.

"We'll need to get quite close to the sleigh to reach it," Rachel whispered to Kirsty.

Luckily, as the two girls reached the sleigh, the goblin had his back to them. He was still searching busily for a switch, so Rachel cautiously reached in towards the Magic Card.

Her hand was centimetres from the shimmering envelope when suddenly the goblin gave a triumphant cry.

"Ooh, I've got a brilliant idea!" he  shouted, spinning round so that Rachel, Kirsty and Chrissie had to duck quickly behind the side of the sleigh out of sight. The goblin picked up the Magic Card. "Christmas card, do the deed and send me a speedy Christmas steed!" he yelled.

"Oh, no!" Chrissie cried in dismay, "He's made another Christmas wish!"

There was a second burst of golden sparks and a magnificent reindeer appeared at the front of the sleigh. Harnessed and ready to go, he pawed the ground impatiently, shaking his antlers.

"Hurrah!" The goblin clapped his hands with glee. "Take me to Jack Frost's ice castle!"

The reindeer galloped off eagerly, and the sleigh whizzed off down the country lane, its golden bells jingling as the goblin whooped with delight.

The girls and Chrissie stared miserably after it.

"This is a disaster!" Chrissie groaned. "Somehow we *must* catch up with that sleigh and get my Magic Card back!"

Stop that Sleigh!

"I'll turn you into fairies," Chrissie told the girls. "Then we can fly after the goblin as fast as we can."

Rachel and Kirsty nodded, and a shower of fairy magic and tiny presents from Chrissie's wand instantly transformed them into fairies with silvery wings on their backs.

"Follow that sleigh!" Chrissie called, swooping through the air after the goblin. Rachel and Kirsty followed, their wings beating so hard that they were just a blur.

At first it was hard work because the goblin was so far ahead. But Chrissie and the girls were so determined that, slowly, they began to close on the speeding sleigh.

"I think we're catching them!" Kirsty

panted after a few minutes.

"Yes, but what then?" Rachel puffed. "We need a plan! It's a pity we didn't get a chance to buy the mince pies, we could have used them to get the goblin's attention."

"Oh!" Kirsty exclaimed, "You've just given me an idea, Rachel. Maybe Chrissie could magic up something that *reindeer* like to eat, and we could use that to lead the reindeer where *we*

want him to go!"

"Well, reindeer love carrots," Chrissie informed them with a smile. "I could magic up a big, juicy carrot."

"And if we can get the reindeer to follow the carrot, I know where we can lead him," Rachel added eagerly.

"We'd better hurry," Kirsty pointed out as they finally caught up with the sleigh, "before it gets away from us again!"

Chrissie pointed her wand at the reindeer and a stream of sparkles swirled towards him. The next moment a big, fat orange carrot appeared, floating in mid air just out of the reindeer's reach. The reindeer gave a snort of delight and strained forward to gobble the carrot up, but fairy magic kept the carrot just a little way ahead of him.

"Brilliant, Chrissie!" Rachel whispered. "Now, we need to move the carrot *that* way, along the bridle path."

And she pointed at a twisting track that led away from the lane and across the fields. Chrissie waved her wand and the carrot floated off along the path.

"Hey!" the goblin shrieked as the reindeer swerved off the road to follow the carrot. "I don't want to go *this* way!"

But the reindeer took no notice. He dashed after the carrot, hurtling eagerly round a sharp bend in the bridle path, while the goblin yelled with fury.

"Look, Chrissie!" Rachel said, pointing ahead of them. "Do you see that stream down in the ditch? Can you lead the reindeer through the water?"

Chrissie lifted her wand and a stream of magic sparkles made the carrot float off the path and into the ditch. The reindeer raced after it down the slope.

"Stop!" yelled the goblin as the sleigh plunged into the ditch behind the reindeer. As it hit the bottom of the ditch, the sleigh tipped right up, hurling the goblin out of his seat.

"Help!" shouted the goblin as he landed in the water with a loud *SPLASH!*

Reindeer Returned

As the goblin floundered in the stream, Chrissie waved her wand and the carrot stopped in mid air. The reindeer immediately grabbed the carrot in his teeth and started munching happily.

Quickly, Rachel, Kirsty and Chrissie swooped down to look for the Magic Card. Kirsty spotted it, lying on the

floor of the sleigh amongst some
cushions, where it had fallen when the
sleigh tipped up. Chrissie pointed her
wand at the shimmering envelope lying
on the pile of cushions and it whirled
up into the air, shrinking down to its
Fairyland size as it did so. Then it
floated over to Chrissie, straight into
her hand.

"My Magic Card is safe!" Chrissie announced, smiling at Rachel and Kirsty as she turned them back to their normal size. "Thank you, girls."

Meanwhile the goblin was climbing out of the ditch, shivering and grumbling. He began jumping from one foot to the other, trying to get warm.

"I'm cold and wet!" the goblin complained, glaring at Chrissie and the girls. "And it's all *your* fault! What are you going to do about it?"

"Well, *I'm* going back to Fairyland with my Magic Card," said Chrissie cheerfully. "Maybe you should go back to Goblin Grotto."

The goblin looked
furious. He blew
a very loud raspberry
and stalked off
through the snow,
grumbling to himself.

"I think we'd better return this sleigh
to Rachel's street and turn it into
a postbox again," Chrissie said with
a grin. "But first things first," she went
on, patting the reindeer who'd now
finished his carrot. "It's time for you to
go back to Santa."

Chrissie dropped a kiss on the
reindeer's nose and then
pointed her wand at
him. He vanished
instantly in a mist
of fairy magic.

"But how will we get the sleigh back to my street without the reindeer?" asked Rachel.

"With fairy magic, of course!" Chrissie cried. "Climb aboard, girls."

Rachel and Kirsty jumped into the sleigh. Then Chrissie waved her wand and glittering fairy dust lifted the sleigh out of the ditch and sent it zooming off towards Tippington. Rachel and Kirsty

loved the feel of gliding over the snow, with the frosty air whipping at their cheeks, and they were bright-eyed and beaming when the sleigh finally came to a halt.

"Time for the sleigh to become a postbox again!" Chrissie announced, as the girls climbed out. With one flick of her wrist, the sleigh vanished, and the red postbox was in its place. Another wave of Chrissie's wand and all the cards still lying on the snowy ground picked themselves up and posted themselves through the slot.

"You've been a great help, girls!" Chrissie said gratefully. "I couldn't have done it without you." Then her little face suddenly became very serious. "Now I need to ask a very big favour," she said solemnly. "If I take the Magic  Card back to Fairyland, it won't be able to work its magic in the human world over Christmas. But if I put the card somewhere else in *your* world, the goblins might find it again! Rachel, do you think you could hide the card somewhere in your house and keep it safe? I'll come back for it in the New Year."

Rachel nodded and grinned. "Of course I can, Chrissie. And my house is the perfect hiding place because my dog, Buttons, is at home most of the time, and the goblins are terrified of him!"

Kirsty laughed. "Oh, yes, of course! The goblins won't dare poke around your house while Buttons is there."

Chrissie did a little twirl of delight in the air. "Oh, thank you!" she cried, clapping her hands. "I knew I could count on you, girls." And, with that, she carefully handed the tiny Magic Card over to Rachel for safe-keeping.

58

"I'll fly straight back to Fairyland now and tell the King and Queen!" Chrissie said happily. "But don't forget to keep an eye out for goblins trying to steal my Magic Spoon and my Magic Carol Sheet, will you?"

"We won't," Rachel cried.

"Yes, don't worry, we won't let Jack Frost spoil Christmas!" Kirsty agreed, and she and Rachel waved as Chrissie vanished in a swirl of sparkles.

A Spoonful
of Magic

Contents

All Mixed Up

"Good morning, girls!" Mrs Walker said as she popped her head round Rachel's bedroom door. "It's time for breakfast."

"OK, Mum," Rachel replied with a yawn. Across the other side of the room, Kirsty was just waking up too.

"Once you've had your cereal, you can help me make the Christmas

pudding!" said Mrs Walker with
a smile.

"Oh, yum!" Kirsty said, sitting up in
bed as Rachel's mum went out. "I *love*
Christmas pudding!"

"But the pudding won't taste very
nice if the goblins get hold of
Chrissie's Magic Spoon," Rachel
pointed out. "The spoon is what
makes Christmas food taste delicious,
remember? I hope Chrissie's hidden
it somewhere really safe!"

The girls showered and dressed and then hurried downstairs and ate their breakfast. Then Mrs Walker began setting out the ingredients for the pudding on the kitchen table.

"Rachel, could you get the big mixing-bowl out of the cupboard, please?" she asked. "And, Kirsty, could you bring the scales? They're on the counter next to the cooker."

Rachel and Kirsty collected the equipment and brought it over to Mrs Walker.

"What goes into the mixing bowl first, Mum?" Rachel asked eagerly.

Mrs Walker reached for the flour but then stopped suddenly, shaking her head. "I've forgotten the most important thing!" she said with a smile. "We must have a spoon to stir the  pudding mixture." And she went over to a drawer and took out a wooden spoon with a pretty golden band around its handle.

"I don't remember seeing this spoon before," Mrs Walker remarked, looking at it curiously. "Your dad must have bought it, Rachel. Anyway, girls, it's a Christmas tradition to make a secret wish as you stir the pudding."

Rachel and Kirsty smiled. They knew all about Christmas wishes after meeting Chrissie the Wish Fairy yesterday.

"OK, girls, first we put the dry ingredients into the bowl, like the flour, sugar and raisins," Mrs Walker went on. "And then in go the eggs and milk."

Kirsty and Rachel helped to weigh out the ingredients and put them in the bowl.

"Now you have to stir the mixture and make a wish," said Rachel's mum. "But don't tell anyone what it is, or it won't come true!" She handed the wooden spoon to Kirsty. "Here you are, Kirsty, you can go first."

Kirsty stirred the sticky mixture. *I wish that the goblins won't get away with Chrissie's Magic Spoon!* she wished to herself. Then she handed the spoon to Rachel. Her friend stirred the pudding and made a secret wish, too, and then Rachel's mum had a go. Finally, they

poured the mixture into a pudding
basin and Mrs Walker put the basin in
a pan of hot water on the stove.

"Oh, there's Buttons!" Rachel said
with a grin as they heard a frantic
scrabbling at the kitchen door. Rachel's
mum opened it and Buttons, the
Walkers' shaggy dog, bounded in
from the hall, tail wagging.

"He's getting excited because it's time for his walk," Rachel pointed out. "Shall Kirsty and I take him?"

"No, don't worry, I'll go. I need to go to the post office," Mrs Walker replied. "Will you keep an eye on the Christmas pudding, girls? You mustn't touch the pan, though, because it's very hot."

"We won't touch it," Rachel promised. "I'll get Dad from the study if there's a problem."

Mrs Walker nodded, put Buttons on the lead, and then the two of them set off.

Rachel turned to Kirsty. "Shall we go upstairs and make some paper chains to decorate the living room?" she suggested. "We can check on the pudding every so often."

"Great idea," Kirsty agreed, and the girls hurried upstairs. "I can't help worrying about Chrissie's Magic Spoon and Magic Carol Sheet," Rachel  confided as they sat on her bed making the paper chains.

"I hope they're safely hidden from the goblins."

"Me too," said Kirsty, tearing open another packet of multi-coloured paper strips. As she did so, a mass of glittering sparkles shot out of the packet and shimmered in the air around the girls.

"Oh!" Kirsty gasped in surprise. Then she and Rachel exchanged a grin, because there, amidst the glitter and tiny sparkly presents, hovered Chrissie the Wish Fairy.

Too Many Cooks

"Hi, girls!" Chrissie cried, smiling at their surprise. "It's me!"

"Hi, Chrissie!" both girls chorused.

"Wow! Look at these paper strips, Rachel!" Kirsty exclaimed in delight, holding one up. "They're all sparkly now!"

Chrissie nodded. "Now your

paper chains will look even more Christmassy!" she declared. "Girls, I've come to check on my Magic Spoon, to make sure it's still safely hidden. Will you show it to me?"

Rachel and Kirsty looked at each other in confusion.

"We don't have the spoon!" Rachel pointed out.

"We don't even know where it is!" added Kirsty.

"Well, I'll tell you," Chrissie said with a huge grin. "I left the spoon in your kitchen, Rachel!"

Rachel's and Kirsty's eyes widened in surprise.

"I knew the spoon would be safe with Buttons around," Chrissie went on. "The goblins are terrified of him!"

Kirsty turned to Rachel. "Remember that wooden spoon we used to stir the Christmas pudding?" Kirsty said excitedly. "The one with the gold band around the handle? Your mum said she hadn't seen it before!"

"Is *that* your Magic Spoon, Chrissie?" Rachel asked.

Chrissie nodded happily.

"Oh, no!" Kirsty said suddenly, clapping her hand to her mouth. "Rachel's mum has taken Buttons out for a walk. The Magic Spoon is downstairs

with no one to guard it!"

"Let's go and make sure it's OK,"
Rachel suggested. "We can check the
pudding at the same time."

The girls hurried downstairs with
Chrissie flying along beside them. Rachel
opened the kitchen door.

"Oh!" Rachel, Kirsty and Chrissie all
gasped in horror as they stared around.
The pudding was still boiling merrily

away, but the kitchen was not as they had left it. The bag of flour had been knocked over and the floor was now completely covered in the white powder, but that was not all. The raisins were scattered across the floor and the counter tops, the walls were splattered with eggs, and the milk bottle had fallen over and was spinning wildly on its side, sending droplets of milk everywhere.

Suddenly, the girls heard the sound of scuffling from underneath the kitchen table. The next moment, two goblins tumbled out, rolling across the floor and getting covered in flour. One of them was clutching the Magic Spoon.

"Give me that spoon!" the bigger goblin bellowed as they crashed into one of the chairs and sent it flying.

"Shan't!" the other goblin retorted, holding the spoon out of his reach.

They rolled across the floor again and
banged into one of the
table legs. The empty
bag of flour fell off
the table and landed
neatly over the
bigger goblin's head.
"Help!" he
spluttered. "I can't see!"

"Teehee!" the goblin with the spoon
chuckled gleefully. He jumped to his

feet to escape, but
immediately skidded
on some spilt milk
and went flying
across the kitchen.
"Ow!" he yelled as
he crashed into one
of the cupboards.

The bigger goblin pulled the bag off his head, his face now white instead of green. Then he rushed across the kitchen, dived on top of the other goblin and began trying to pull the spoon out of his hand again.

"That's enough!" Chrissie called sternly, fluttering into the middle of

the kitchen. "Stop fighting this instant! Tidy up the Walkers' kitchen! And give me back my Magic Spoon!"

Goblins in Hiding

The goblins shrieked with fright at the sound of Chrissie's voice. Quickly, the one holding the Magic Spoon hid it behind his back. "What spoon?" he asked innocently.

"The one behind your back, silly!" the other goblin said impatiently.

"Oh, *you're* the silly one!" shouted the goblin with the spoon, dancing up and down in a rage. "I was trying to hide it, you idiot!"

The bigger goblin stuck his bottom lip out sulkily. "Well, how was I supposed to know *that*?" he grumbled.

Rachel and Kirsty tried not to smile and Chrissie winked at them.

"Give me my spoon, please," Chrissie said firmly.

The goblins shook their heads and backed away as Rachel, Kirsty and Chrissie approached.

"That spoon doesn't belong to you!" Rachel added. "Give it back."

The goblins looked extremely nervous and started muttering to each other. Then, as Rachel and Kirsty came even closer, the bigger goblin skipped one way and the goblin with the spoon ran the other. They dodged around the girls and darted straight out of the door.

"We've got to stop them," Rachel said, following the goblins out into the hall. "Oh, no, they're going upstairs. I just hope Dad doesn't hear them!"

Kirsty, Rachel and Chrissie hurried up the stairs after the goblins. But when they reached the landing, the goblins were nowhere to be seen.

"Where *can* they be?" Kirsty asked anxiously.

Suddenly the door of the study  opened and Mr Walker looked out. Immediately Chrissie fluttered out of sight behind a pot plant on the landing.

"Is everything OK, girls?" he asked. "I can hear a lot of running up and down the stairs!"

"We're just playing a game, Dad," Rachel replied.

"That's fine, but be careful," Mr Walker said with a smile. "I'll just check on the Christmas pudding while you're playing."

Rachel's heart sank as she thought about the state of the kitchen and she exchanged a panicky look with Kirsty. "Erm, the pudding's fine!" Kirsty assured Mr Walker quickly. "Rachel and I have just had a look."

"Oh, OK," said Mr Walker. "What game are you playing, by the way?"

"Um, hide and seek," Rachel told him.

"Well, have fun," Mr Walker called before closing his study door.

"Phew, that was close!" Rachel whispered as Chrissie popped out from behind the plant.

"Girls, we *must* get my spoon back or all the Christmas food will taste awful," the little fairy said with an anxious frown. "And none of the wishes people make when they're stirring their Christmas puddings will come true!"

"Don't worry, Chrissie," Kirsty said in a determined voice. "We'll find the goblins!"

"Let's start looking for them in my bedroom," Rachel suggested.

The girls went into Rachel's room, followed closely by Chrissie. Quickly they searched behind the curtains and the door, and then they looked in the wardrobe.

"They're not here," Rachel said, disappointed.

"I'm not so sure," Chrissie whispered. "Look!" And she pointed across the room with her wand. Rachel's and Kirsty's eyes widened. There, poking out from under Rachel's bed, they could just see one green hand.

Kirsty, who was closest, jumped forwards and grabbed it. "Got you!" she yelled triumphantly.

Green Fingers

Kirsty tugged at the hand, but
something wasn't quite right. The
hand felt soft and fluffy. She frowned
and looked down. Instead of pulling
a goblin out from under the bed, Kirsty
found herself holding a stuffed toy frog.

"Oh, that's mine!" Rachel exclaimed,
looking a bit embarrassed. She took the

toy frog from Kirsty and sat it on the

bed. "I bought it because I thought it looked a bit like Bertram!" Kirsty grinned as she remembered their frog footman friend from Fairyland. "Your frog's lovely, Rachel," she laughed. "But he's not as talkative as the *real* Bertram!"

"I don't think the goblins are here, do you, girls?" asked Chrissie, checking under Kirsty's bed on the other side of the room.

"Let's try my mum and dad's bedroom next," Rachel suggested.

The three friends hurried next door.

Chrissie looked under the bed while Kirsty and Rachel searched behind the furniture.

Suddenly Rachel froze. She had just caught a glimpse of green out of the corner of her eye. Slowly she turned around. There was definitely something green sticking out slightly from behind the bedroom door.

Putting her finger to her lips, Rachel
pointed it out to Kirsty and Chrissie.
They nodded, and then all three of
them crept quietly across the room.

"Found you!" Rachel cried, springing
forwards. But her face fell when she
pulled the door back to see nothing
but a green dressing-gown hanging
on a hook.

"Oh, I really thought we had them then!" Kirsty sighed. "Where else can they be?"

Rachel frowned. "Well, they can't be in the study because Dad's in there," she pointed out. "That only leaves the bathroom, unless the goblins have managed to sneak out of the house."

Chrissie shook her head. "No, I don't think they've done that," she said. "I can sense that my spoon is still close by. Let's try the bathroom."

They rushed along the landing and Rachel opened the bathroom door.

The room looked perfectly normal and Rachel couldn't see anything out of the ordinary as she scanned it carefully.

Suddenly a shaft of wintry sunlight shone through the window and lit up the room. Immediately, Kirsty gave a tiny gasp and pointed at the bathtub. There, behind the shower curtain, was the silhouette of two goblins, their long pointy noses casting a very clear shadow. Kirsty, Rachel and Chrissie glanced at each other, but they didn't dare say anything in case the goblins hiding in the bath heard them.

They all stood very still, wondering what to do next.

As Kirsty stared at the shower, she was suddenly struck by an idea. She looked at Chrissie and then pointed at the shower head. Chrissie's face lit up and she winked at the girls. Then she waved her wand at the shower, which was directly above the goblins' heads...

A Goblin Wash-out

A stream of red sparkles and tiny presents shot out of Chrissie's wand and surrounded the shower head. Immediately the shower sprang to life and a jet of water shot straight out onto the goblins.

"Aaarghh! Let me out of here!" the bigger goblin roared, pulling back the shower curtain. "It's freezing!"

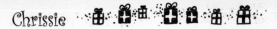

"I'm getting soaked!" screeched the
one with the spoon. "I'm going home!"
They both tried to scramble out of the
shower but they got tangled up in the
curtain and landed back in the bath.
Moaning, grumbling and dripping
wet, they eventually managed to
clamber out. They were so keen to
get away from the cold water that

the smallest goblin
didn't even notice
that he'd dropped
the Magic Spoon
on the bathroom
floor. Shivering and
shaking, the goblins

dashed over to the door, hurtled out of
the room and down the stairs.

"We did it, girls!" Chrissie exclaimed
as Rachel picked up the Magic Spoon.
"You were great. Thank you for all
your help!"

Kirsty and Rachel smiled as Chrissie waved her wand again. This time a stream of glittery fairy dust shrank the spoon down to its Fairyland size. It floated through the air towards Chrissie and she took it with a huge smile.

"Now everyone's Christmas dinner will taste wonderful, and the wishes people make when they stir their Christmas puddings will come true!" Chrissie said happily, hugging the Magic Spoon to her.

"Are you going to take the spoon back to Fairyland to keep it safe?" asked Kirsty.

Chrissie's face fell. "I can't," she said. "If I take it away from the human world, it won't be able to work its Christmas magic," she explained. "I need to find a new hiding place."

Kirsty looked thoughtful. "I could keep it and take home with me tomorrow," she offered. "The goblins won't know I've got it and my cat, Pearl, doesn't like goblins, so she'll make quite a good guard cat!"

"That's great! Thank you," Chrissie cried happily, handing the tiny Magic Spoon over to Kirsty, who put it carefully in her pocket.

"Now, there's one more thing I must do before I go back to Fairyland," she added, fluttering out of the bathroom. Curious, Rachel and Kirsty followed the little fairy down to the kitchen.

"Oh, I forgot about the mess that the goblins made!" Rachel groaned as she and Kirsty stood in the doorway. "Mum isn't going to be very pleased!"

"Don't worry," Chrissie said with a smile, "a little fairy magic will

soon sort this kitchen out."

Rachel and Kirsty watched, fascinated, as Chrissie worked her magic. The flour swirled up from the floor and back into its bag in a clean white cloud. The milk flowed backwards into the bottle, which immediately righted itself. And the eggs peeled themselves off the wall and rolled back into their broken eggshells which then became whole again.

By the time the last magic sparkle had drifted away, the kitchen was spotless and all the ingredients were back on the table in a neat little row.

"Thank you, Chrissie," Rachel said gratefully. "It looks even cleaner than it did before!"

"Your mum and Buttons will be back soon so I must be going," Chrissie said. "You've been brilliant, girls, but Jack Frost and his goblins will still be trying to spoil Christmas. I'm relying on you to help me stop them!"

"We'll do our best, Chrissie!" Kirsty promised, and Rachel nodded eagerly.

"Goodbye then, girls," Chrissie called, waving her wand as she vanished in a burst of glittery red fairy dust.

Kirsty turned to Rachel. "You know, when we stirred the Christmas pudding and made a wish?" she said. "Well, my wish came true!"

"Really? So did mine!" Rachel replied. "I wished that Chrissie's spoon wouldn't be stolen by the goblins!"

"I wished for exactly the same thing!"
Kirsty laughed. The girls looked at
each other in delight.

"It's Christmas Eve tomorrow,"
Rachel pointed out. "And I bet Jack
Frost and his goblins will be looking
for Chrissie's Magic Carol Sheet!"

Kirsty nodded. Then she grinned. "Well, we'll be ready for them!" she said in a determined voice.

Chrissie's
Christmas Carol

Contents

Rachel and Kirsty Go Carolling

"*We wish you a merry Christmas,*"
Rachel and Kirsty sang. "*And a happy
new year.*"

It was Christmas Eve, and the girls
were out with a group of friends and
neighbours, singing carols to raise
money for charity. Although it was
a cold and frosty evening, the girls

were wrapped up warmly and really enjoying themselves.

"I think that's my favourite carol!" Kirsty exclaimed as they finished singing, and received a huge round of applause. They were in a small cul-de-sac and people had come out of their houses to listen to the carols.

"That's because it's all about wishes," Rachel said in a low voice. "Talking of wishes, we *must* keep a look-out for goblins! They're still after Chrissie's Magic Carol Sheet."

Kirsty sighed. "We mustn't let those goblins steal it, or Christmas carols won't be able to spread their Christmas

cheer and good wishes everywhere."

"And that would spoil Christmas!" Rachel agreed. "Let's just hope we can find the Magic Carol Sheet, and keep it safe from goblins, before your parents come and pick you up later tonight."

Kirsty nodded.

"Now we're going to sing our last

carol before we move on to Tippington Lane," announced Andrew, the lead carol singer. "Please turn to *Silent Night*." Everyone flicked

through their carol sheets to find the right one. As they did, Rachel suddenly noticed a very faint red sparkle to her left. Curiously, she glanced sideways.

A lady named Isabelle was standing
there, and Rachel drew in her breath
sharply as she saw red sparkles
dancing at the edges of one of
Isabelle's carol sheets.

Those are fairy sparkles! Rachel
thought, excitedly. She nudged Kirsty.
"Look at Isabelle's carol sheets," Rachel
whispered, as everyone started singing
again. "One of them is sparkling!"

Kirsty stared hard and her eyes widened in amazement. "It must be Chrissie's Magic Carol Sheet!" she breathed. "Luckily, Isabelle hasn't noticed those sparkles!"

"We'd better stick close to her and keep an eye on that sheet," Rachel went on. "That way we know it's safe."

The carol finished, and Andrew led the singers on to their next stop as the watching crowd applauded loudly. Kirsty and Rachel were careful to stay near Isabelle as they headed down a little lane, lined with pretty cottages.

As Andrew knocked on the doors one
by one and the group sang their carols
to each household, Kirsty and Rachel
were careful to keep the Magic
Carol Sheet in sight the whole time.
Everyone in the cottages was very
friendly and gave lots of money to
them for charity.

As they reached the bottom of the lane, Andrew pointed to the last cottage. "That's funny!" he said with a frown. "The lights are on in Mrs Patterson's house, but she told me she was going away for Christmas." He scratched his chin thoughtfully. "She must have decided to stay at home. Let's go and sing her a carol."

They walked over to Mrs Patterson's cottage and knocked on the door, which was decorated with a beautiful Christmas wreath of holly and ivy.

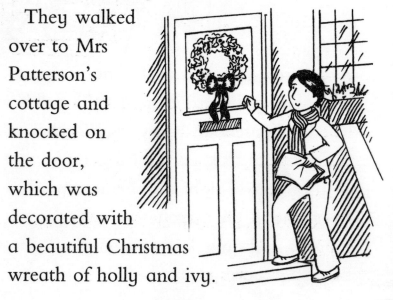

128

The door was flung open by a very short, elderly man with a long white beard. "What do you want?" he snapped, scowling. Rachel and Kirsty glanced at each other in surprise. Until now, everyone had been really pleased to see them.

Andrew was looking shocked too. "We've come to see if Mrs Patterson would like us to sing her a carol," he explained.

The old man's face lit up. "Did you say a *carol*?"

Andrew nodded.

"I'm Mrs Patterson's brother," the old man said, suddenly sounding much friendlier. "My sister's in bed with a cold, but I'd *love* to hear a carol!"

"OK," Andrew agreed with a smile. "We'll sing extra loudly so that Mrs Patterson can hear us upstairs." He turned to the rest of the group. "Let's sing *We Wish You a Merry Christmas*."

Everyone flicked through their carol

sheets to *We Wish You a Merry Christmas.* Rachel nudged Kirsty. Isabelle had put the sparkly sheet at the top of her pile. "Look, Kirsty!" Rachel whispered, *"We Wish You a Merry Christmas* is the Magic Carol Sheet!"

Kirsty nodded, but she was distracted by the old man, who was scanning the carol singers eagerly, as if he was looking for someone in particular.

When his gaze fell on the Magic
Carol Sheet, he grinned and danced
a little jig of delight on the doorstep.
As he did so, his beard slipped for an
instant, revealing a very long and
very pointy nose.

Kirsty and Rachel gasped with dismay. "That's not Mrs Patterson's brother!" Rachel whispered. "It's a goblin!"

Girls Go Into Action!

"OK, everyone," Andrew called, "I'll count you in. One, two, three..."

"Oh, this is lovely!" the girls heard the goblin sigh as everyone began to sing. "I love songs about wishes!"

Anxiously, Rachel and Kirsty started to edge in front of Isabelle to protect the Magic Carol Sheet, but as they

moved, the goblin
suddenly lunged
forward from
the doorstep
and snatched
the carol sheet
from Isabelle's
hand. Then he
dashed back into
the cottage and
slammed the door.

Shocked, everyone stopped singing
and stared at each other in
bewilderment.

"That's strange!" Andrew said,
bemusedly. "What did he do *that* for?"

"Knock on the door, Andrew, and
ask him to return it," Isabelle suggested.
Andrew rapped at the door.

"What are we going to do, Rachel?"
Kirsty whispered. "The goblin isn't
going to give the carol sheet back."

Sure enough, the goblin
didn't answer
Andrew's knock,
and after a few
moments, Andrew
shrugged in defeat.
"Mrs Patterson's
brother must really
want that carol sheet!"

he remarked. "Well, let's move on.
Isabelle, you can share my carol sheet
when we sing that one next time."

As the carol singers moved off, Rachel
hurried over to Andrew. "Kirsty and
I will knock once more and see if we
can get the carol sheet back," she said.

"OK, girls," Andrew agreed, "but don't be long."

The girls waited until the carol singers were further down the lane. Then Kirsty knocked loudly on the door.

"Come out!" Rachel called. "We know you're not Mrs Patterson's brother!"

"You're a goblin!" Kirsty shouted. "Now, give us back the carol sheet – it doesn't belong to you!"

But the door remained firmly closed.

"What shall we do now?" asked Rachel.

Suddenly the girls saw red fairy sparkles beginning to fizz around the Christmas wreath on the door in front of them. As they watched, Chrissie zipped out from amongst the leaves.

"I saw everything that happened, girls!" she cried. "Now let's get my Magic Carol Sheet back from that naughty goblin!"

Chrissie tapped briskly on the cottage door with her wand. Even though her wand was tiny, her fairy magic made it sound like ten fists were pounding on the door at once.

"Go away!" shouted the goblin, but he sounded nervous. "I'm sending Jack Frost a message to let him know that I've got the Magic Carol Sheet, and he'll come to collect it himself, so you'd better leave me alone!"

Chrissie, Rachel and Kirsty looked at each other in concern.

"If Jack Frost gets his hands on my carol sheet, my Christmas Wish Magic won't work properly," Chrissie sighed.

"We *must* get the carol sheet back before Jack Frost turns up!"

"But how can we get into the cottage?" asked Kirsty.

Rachel scanned the house and noticed that it had a chimney.  "There's no smoke coming out of the chimney pot," she pointed out. "If Chrissie turns us into fairies we could fly down the chimney."

"Like Santa Claus," Kirsty said with a grin. "But with wings!"

"That's a great idea!" Chrissie said, instantly looking more cheerful. "Ready, girls?"

Rachel and Kirsty put their carol
sheets down on the doorstep and
nodded. Chrissie waved her wand and
transformed the girls into tiny, sparkling
fairies. Immediately the three friends
zipped up to the roof and hovered
above the chimney. Then they plunged
inside. It was very dark.

"It's a bit spooky!" Kirsty whispered.

"I know," Chrissie agreed. "I hope we're not getting all sooty."

Rachel, who was a little ahead of the other two, could now see a light at the bottom of the chimney. As she stared downwards, she suddenly saw a thin, silvery ribbon of smoke, twisting its way up towards her. Her heart skipped a beat; had the goblin lit a fire in the grate?

But as the smoke got closer, she saw that it was actually an ice-cold mist, and a little white envelope was being carried along inside it. Rachel gasped as she glimpsed the name on the front of the envelope: it was addressed to Jack Frost!

To: Jack Frost, Ice Castle,

"Did you see that?" Rachel exclaimed.

"Yes, the goblin has sent his message to Jack Frost!" Chrissie replied, watching the envelope shoot out of the chimney. "There's no time to lose, girls. Jack Frost will be here very soon!"

An Icy Guest

As the three friends reached the bottom of the chimney, they heard a terrible wailing noise.

"What's that?" Rachel whispered. "It's horrible!"

They hovered in the fireplace and peeped into the lounge. They could see the goblin in front of them, standing on a brightly coloured rug in the middle of the room. He had the carol sheet in his hand and was singing *We Wish You a Merry Christmas*, loudly and tunelessly.

"That's the worst singing I've ever heard!" Chrissie groaned. "Let's grab the carol sheet back and get out of here!"

"We need a distraction," Rachel whispered.

Kirsty glanced down at the fireplace below and had an idea. "Chrissie, could you start a fire?" Kirsty asked. "The goblin will be surprised, and while he's distracted, we can try to grab the carol sheet."

Chrissie nodded. "We'd better move before I start the fire," she said.

Chrissie, Rachel and Kirsty flew silently out of the fireplace and hid behind a chair.

Then Chrissie pointed her wand at the

grate and flames
instantly leapt up,
filling the room
with a warm
golden glow.
"Oh!" the goblin
exclaimed. He
stopped singing
and hurried over
to the fire, tucking
the carol sheet under
his arm and holding
his hands out to the warmth.

Seemingly mesmerised by the
dancing flames, he sank slowly into an
armchair next to the fire, placed the
carol sheet in his lap, and dozed off.

"Now!" Kirsty whispered.

The friends darted out of their
hiding-place and across the room. As
the goblin began to snore, they hovered
behind his armchair and Kirsty stretched
out her hand towards the Magic
Carol Sheet.

But just as her fingers brushed it, the
fire crackled loudly, waking the goblin.
He immediately caught a glimpse of
Kirsty and gave a shriek of rage,
snatching the carol sheet out of her reach.

"Pesky fairies!" he shouted, leaping to his feet and swiping at Chrissie and the girls so that they had to zip smartly out of the way.

The goblin hopped furiously up and down on the rug, holding the carol sheet behind his back. "You pesky fairies don't scare me!" he sneered. "Jack Frost will deal with you!"

"Give us the carol sheet, please!"

Chrissie said. "Or Christmas will be ruined!"

But the goblin just stuck his tongue out rudely.

Suddenly, despite the blazing fire, Rachel and Kirsty began to shiver.

"Look, there are sheets of ice spreading across the windowpanes!" Rachel stammered through

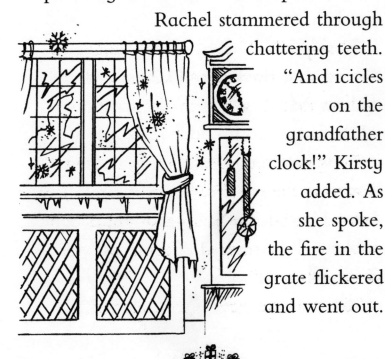

chattering teeth. "And icicles on the grandfather clock!" Kirsty added. As she spoke, the fire in the grate flickered and went out.

"Jack Frost is on his way!" Chrissie whispered anxiously.

Kirsty knew that they had to do something to get the carol sheet back before Jack Frost arrived. She looked around desperately for inspiration, and her eye was caught by the bright colours of the rug that the goblin was standing on.

Quickly she pointed at the rug, hoping that Rachel and Chrissie would understand.

Her friends both nodded,  and, as Kirsty and Rachel swooped down towards the goblin, Chrissie pointed her wand at the rug.

A rush of sparkles surrounded the rug and pulled it sharply out from under the goblin's feet. With a squeal of surprise, he landed on his bottom with a bump, and Kirsty and Rachel grabbed the carol  sheet from his flailing hands.

"Let's get out of here!" Chrissie shouted, pointing her wand at the door.

But as they whizzed towards it, the door flew open, and Jack Frost swept into the room on a blast of icy wind.

A Wish in Time

Jack Frost roared with rage as he
spotted the girls holding the Magic
Carol Sheet.

"That belongs to me!" he shouted,
pointing his wand at them.

An ice bolt flew towards Kirsty and
Rachel with deadly speed. They both
managed to jump aside, but the force of

the ice bolt streaking past sent them
tumbling into a corner of the room.

Chrissie rushed over to help the girls,
but Jack Frost sent another ice bolt
flying towards her. Chrissie dodged it,
but it struck the goblin, who was just
staggering up from the floor, and he
was instantly frozen solid.

"Give me that carol sheet!" Jack Frost
bellowed. "Or I'll turn you into fairy

popsicles!" And he advanced on
the girls, shaking his ice wand
threateningly.

Trapped in the corner, Rachel and
Kirsty tried to think fast.

"Quick, girls, make a Christmas
wish!" Chrissie called urgently. "You
have the Magic Carol Sheet, so it's
sure to come true, and it's the only
way to stop Jack Frost!"

Kirsty frowned in thought as Jack Frost drew nearer, and Rachel closed her eyes.

"*Peace and goodwill at Christmas time,*

"*This is my wish as I speak this rhyme!*" Rachel declared.

"*Jack Frost is mean. Jack Frost is vile,*
"*Use Christmas cheer to make him smile!*" Kirsty added quickly.

Jack Frost loomed menacingly over the girls and raised his wand. Had they wished too late?

Suddenly, Jack Frost stopped in his tracks and lowered his wand. "Now, girls, you know the carol sheet doesn't belong to you, or to me," he said, wagging an icy finger at them. "It belongs to Chrissie. You must give it back to her."

Rachel and Kirsty could hardly believe their ears. Behind Jack Frost's back, Chrissie winked at them.

"Oh, yes, we will!" Rachel assured him.

"Good! Now I must go home. I've got lots to do before Christmas," Jack Frost explained. "I have to wrap presents for all my lovely goblin helpers, and I think I'll cook them a delicious Christmas dinner too, as a thank-you for all their hard work."

Rachel and Kirsty exchanged a delighted grin as Jack Frost waved his wand and unfroze the goblin.

"S-sorry I got in the way of your ice bolt!" the goblin stammered, looking terrified.

Jack Frost slapped him on the back so heartily that the goblin almost fell over.

"No, no, it was all *my* fault!" he declared. "Come on, we'll go Christmas shopping and you can choose a lovely present for yourself!"

The goblin's mouth fell open and he looked so shocked that Rachel, Kirsty and Chrissie laughed out loud. Then Jack Frost waved his wand and he and the goblin were whisked from the room by an icy whirlwind.

"Thank you, girls," Chrissie exclaimed happily as she flew over to them, turning them back to their normal size. "Your wish worked beautifully!" She pointed her wand at the carol sheet, and it immediately shrank to its Fairyland size. Then it floated over to Chrissie and she tucked it carefully under her arm.

"It's a shame Jack Frost can't be that nice *all* the time!" Kirsty laughed, and Rachel nodded.

"I don't know how long your wish will last, girls," Chrissie said, "so I must hide my carol sheet safely in your human world."

"Would you like me to hide the carol sheet at my house?" Rachel offered. "The paper is so small now that it will easily fit into the address locket on Buttons' collar. The goblins will never dare take it from there!"

"Oh, that's a marvellous idea!" Chrissie agreed delightedly, handing the Magic Carol Sheet to Rachel. "Thank you."

Rachel tucked the tiny carol sheet carefully into her pocket.

"I'll come and collect all my magic objects at the very end of the year," Chrissie said. "And I'll take you both back to Fairyland for our New Year's

Eve Ball — if you'd like to come."

"We'd love to!" Kirsty and Rachel chorused.

"Well, don't forget to put on your dancing shoes," Chrissie said with a wink. "Now, I must go and tell the King and Queen that all the Christmas Wish items are safe."

The girls nodded. "Goodbye!" they called, waving.

"Thanks again for all your help," Chrissie said. "And keep your eyes open for a little Christmas present. See you on New Year's Eve!"

And, with that, Chrissie disappeared in a cloud of red sparkles.

"We did it!" Kirsty exclaimed happily as they went outside. "We saved Christmas!"

"Yes, and we've had another fantastic fairy adventure!" Rachel agreed, bending down to pick up her carol sheets from the doorstep. But, suddenly, she stopped in surprise, because there, on top of her pile of papers, was a little book with her name on it. Glittering sparkles festooned the cover.

Kirsty had one too. "It's a diary!" she cried in delight, flicking through the pages. "It must be the Christmas present that Chrissie told us about."

"It's going to be a wonderful Christmas," Rachel sighed happily, putting her diary in her pocket.

Kirsty nodded. "And we have a very special present that will always remind us of Chrissie the Wish Fairy!" she said. "Now, let's go and sing some more carols and wish everyone a very merry Christmas."

Win Rainbow Magic Goodies!

There are lots of Rainbow Magic fairies, and we want to know which one is your favourite! Send us a picture of her and tell us in 30 words why she is your favourite and why you like Rainbow Magic books. Each month we will put the entries into a draw and select one winner to receive a Rainbow Magic Sparkly T-shirt and Goody Bag!

Send your entry on a postcard to Rainbow Magic Competition, Orchard Books, 338 Euston Road, London NW1 3BH. Australian readers should email: childrens.books@hachette.com.au New Zealand readers should write to Rainbow Magic Competition, 4 Whetu Place, Mairangi Bay, Auckland NZ. Don't forget to include your name and address. Only one entry per child.

Good luck!

Where the magic begins...

Ruby the Red Fairy

When Rachel and Kirsty meet on a
holiday to Rainspell Island, they have
no idea what magical adventures
lie ahead...

The End of the Rainbow

"Look, Dad!" said Rachel Walker. She pointed across the blue-green sea at the rocky island ahead of them. The ferry was sailing towards it, dipping up and down on the rolling waves. "Is that Rainspell Island?" she asked.

Her dad nodded. "Yes, it is," he said, smiling. "Our holiday is about to begin!"

The waves slapped against the side of the ferry as it bobbed up and down on the water. Rachel felt her heart thump with excitement. She could see white cliffs and emerald green fields on the island. And golden sandy beaches, with rock pools dotted here and there.

Suddenly, a few fat raindrops plopped down on to Rachel's head. "Oh!" she gasped, surprised. The sun was still shining.

Rachel's mum grabbed her hand. "Let's get under cover," she said, leading Rachel inside.

"Isn't that strange?" Rachel said. "Sunshine *and* rain!"

"Let's hope the rain stops before we get off the ferry," said Mr Walker. "Now, where did I put that map of the island?"

Rachel looked out of the window.

A girl was standing alone on the deck. Her hair was wet with raindrops, but she didn't seem to care. She just stared up at the sky...

Have you checked out the

Website at:

www.rainbowmagic.co.uk

There are games, activities and
fun things to do, as well as news
and information about Rainbow
Magic and all of the fairies.